This book
belongs to:

Just imagine . . . growing, **flying,** slee
blowing, **swimming,** eating, playing,
rollerskating, parent-frightening, **read**
falling, **bird-riding,** washing, sailing,
rusting, unravelling, **nibbling,** scari
dinosaur-hunting, chariot-riding, chimr
demonstrating, g-dressing, **jousting,**
rumbling, r nding, clanging, pu
squeaking, **bubbling,** spell-c
charming, rope-climbing, magic-carpe
brewing, **Pegasus-riding,** roaring, **howl**
chomping, leaping, **chewing,** splashin
buzzing, **snorting,** bounding, resting, t
scuttling, scurrying, **jumping,** walkin
tunnelling, digging, fossil-hunting, **burr**
cycling, wheeling, **driving,** unicycling, m
riding, **helicopter-flying,** diving, floatin

, sneezing, walking, **shouting**, chasing, scuing, **shrinking**, writing, climbing, running, biting, drinking, **escaping**, hing, transforming, **wobbling**, melting, **stretching**, popping, time-travelling, sweeping, **spaceship-flying**, evacuating, ng, Viking-meeting, **inventing**, whirring, ng, buzzing, **creaking**, slurping, beeping, ng, wish-granting, bewitching, **snake-**ing, **fire-breathing**, egg-laying, potion-, changing, hanging, racing, **crawling**, swinging, **sliding**, slithering, laughing, ting, munching, nibbling, **ball-chasing**, eeding, cuddling, creeping, exploring, ng, painting, treasure-hunting, **whizzing**, biking, **hang-gliding**, hot-air ballooning, gliding, sinking, discovering, **dreaming**,

For everyone who loves Heffers Children's Bookshop
P.G.

For Lily, Lucy, Emily, Jessica, Florence and Henry
N.S.

First published in 2012 as *Just Imagine*

PUFFIN BOOKS

UK | USA | Canada | Ireland | Australia
India | New Zealand | South Africa

Puffin Books is part of the Penguin Random House group of companies
whose addresses can be found at global.penguinrandomhouse.com.

www.penguin.co.uk   www.puffin.co.uk   www.ladybird.co.uk

 Penguin
Random House
UK

Doubleday edition published 2012
Picture Corgi edition published 2013
This edition published 2018
001

Printed in China

A CIP catalogue record for this book is available from the British Library

ISBN: 978-0-241-33497-3

All correspondence to:
Puffin Books, Penguin Random House Children's,
80 Strand, London WC2R 0RL

YOU
CHOOSE
YOUR DREAMS

Imagine being as big as a house!

Or as tiny as a flea!

Take a look inside this book and decide what you'd like to be.

Nick Sharratt & Pippa Goodhart

PUFFIN

Can you imagine being BIG?

Or would you like to be small?

Imagine being made differently

Imagine being magical

Imagine being an animal,

living in the wild.

Perhaps you'd rather be a pet, belonging to some child.

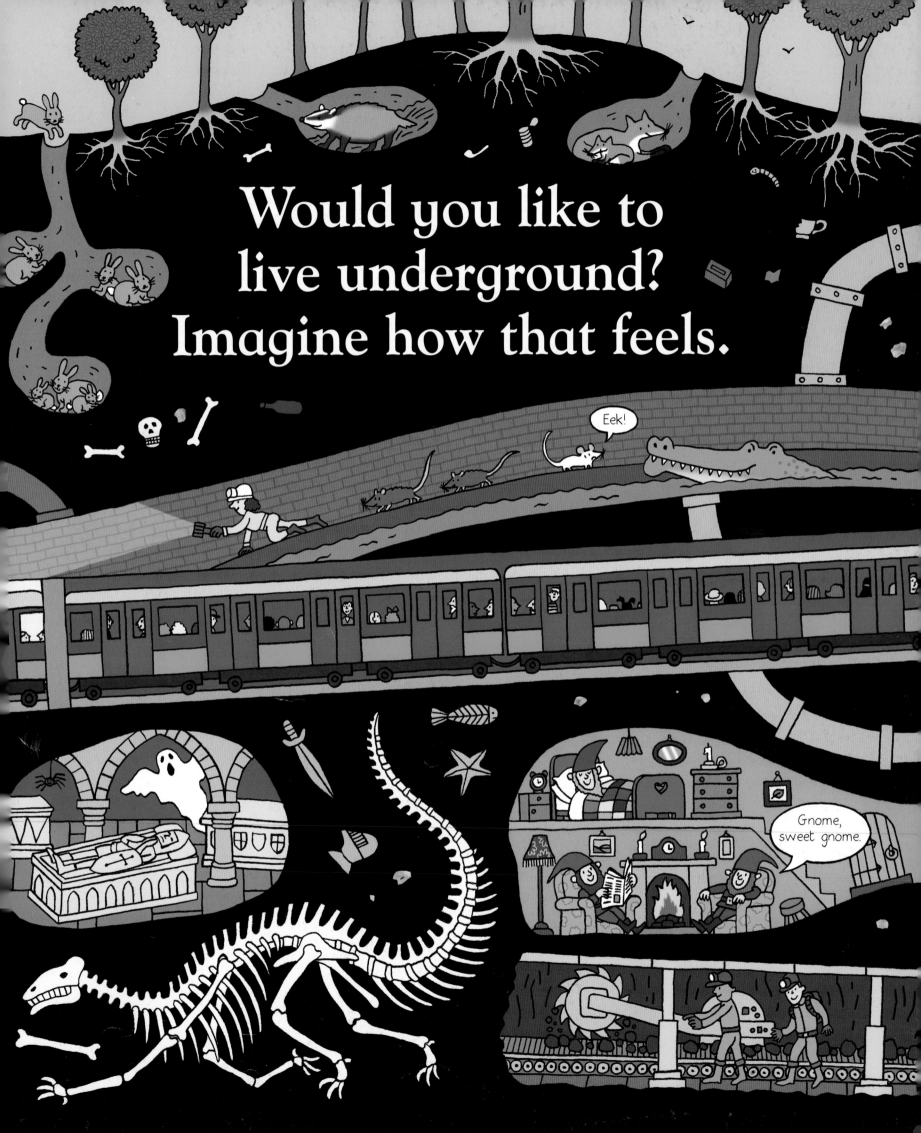

Or would you like to whizz around on some kind of wheels?

Just imagine . . . growing, **flying**, sleep
blowing, **swimming**, eating, playing,
rollerskating, parent-frightening, **readi**
falling, **bird-riding**, washing, sailing, l
rusting, unravelling, **nibbling**, scari
dinosaur-hunting, chariot-riding, chimn
demonstrating, fancy-dressing, **jousting**,
rumbling, **rolling**, grinding, clanging, pu
squeaking, huffing, **bubbling**, spell-co
charming, rope-climbing, magic-carpet
brewing, **Pegasus-riding**, roaring, **howl**
chomping, leaping, **chewing**, splashin
buzzing, **snorting**, bounding, resting, t
scuttling, scurrying, **jumping**, walking
tunnelling, digging, fossil-hunting, **burro**
cycling, wheeling, **driving**, unicycling, m
riding, **helicopter-flying**, diving, floati

, sneezing, walking, **shouting**, chasing, scuing, **shrinking**, writing, climbing, running, biting, drinking, **escaping**, hing, transforming, **wobbling**, melting, stretching, popping, time-travelling, sweeping, **spaceship-flying**, evacuating, ng, Viking-meeting, **inventing**, whirring, ng, buzzing, **creaking**, slurping, beeping, ng, wish-granting, bewitching, **snake-** ing, **fire-breathing**, egg-laying, potion-changing, hanging, racing, **crawling**, winging, **sliding**, slithering, laughing, ing, munching, nibbling, **ball-chasing**, eding, cuddling, creeping, **exploring**, g, painting, treasure-hunting, **whizzing**, biking, **hang-gliding**, hot-air ballooning, liding, sinking, discovering, **dreaming,**

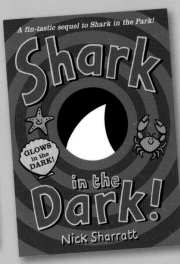

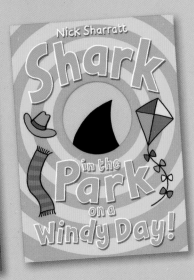

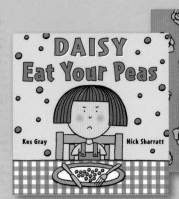

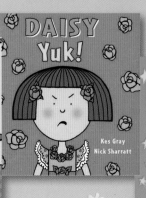

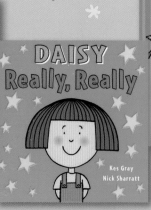

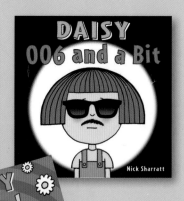

Why not choose
some more books
illustrated by Nick Sharratt?